W9-BMD-840

It was nine o'clock at night when Charlie heard a tap on her bedroom window. At first she thought it was the wind. But then she heard the noise a second time.

Charlie jumped out of bed.

What was that? she thought. *Could it be a ghost?*

The tapping noise came again.

Charlie was scared. She wanted to open the curtains and look out the window. If only she weren't so afraid.

"Grrrrr" came the noise from outside.

Charlie was now panicking. "What'll I do?" she said over and over.

"Grrrrr" the noise sounded again.

Charlie ran out of the room as fast as she could. She bolted down the steps and into the living room.

"What's wrong, Charlotte?" asked her father. "You look like you've seen a ghost."

"I have!" said Charlie. "It's right outside my window!"

Don't miss the other books in
The Kids on the Bus series!

Available from
HarperPaperbacks

6

The Kids on the Bus

THE HAUNTED BUS

Marjorie and Andrew Sharmat

Illustrated by Meredith Johnson

HarperPaperbacks

A Division of HarperCollins*Publishers*

To My Dad,
Mitchell Sharmat
A.R.S.

To My Husband,
Mitchell Sharmat
M.W.S.

HarperPaperbacks   *A Division of* HarperCollins*Publishers*
10 East 53rd Street, New York, N.Y. 10022

Produced by Chardiet Unlimited Inc.
33 West 17th Street, New York, New York 10011.

RL 2.1 IL 007-009
First printing: September 1991

Printed in the United States of America

10 9 8 7 6 5 4 3 2

THE HAUNTED BUS

CHAPTER 1

"Come on, school bus . . . get here now. I'm freezing!"

The bus was late, and Charlie McKee was alone in the cold.

"Gloves," she said shivering. "I have to find my gloves."

Charlie opened her backpack and started throwing books onto the ground.

"I know you gloves are hiding in there and I'm going to find you," she said.

But a minute later, her backpack was empty, and all of her books and papers were lying on the ground. And still no gloves.

Then a cold gust blew her third-grade math notebook open and scattered papers all over the sidewalk. Charlie tried to pick up as many papers as she could, but the wind carried some of them out of her reach.

Cleaning up this mess could take forever,

thought Charlie. *And with my luck, the bus will come before I get these papers picked up.*

Charlie chased more papers down the sidewalk. Then she heard a loud noise.

S-C-R-E-E-C-H!! E-E-E-C-H!!

Charlie looked up. The bus had pulled up to her stop.

Harry the bus driver stepped down from the bus.

"What a disaster," he said as he glanced at the ground. "I think you could use a hand from your favorite bus driver."

Harry was Charlie's favorite bus driver. Actually, he was the *only* bus driver that Charlie knew. Most of the kids on the bus were scared of Harry. But he was always nice to Charlie.

Soon all the papers were back in Charlie's notebook, and her books were in her backpack. Charlie thanked Harry and climbed onto the bus.

Some of the kids made fun of her as she walked to her seat.

"You naughty, naughty girl," said Brian Ray, the sixth grader who loved to pick on younger kids. "If you don't pick up your toys when you're done with them, you won't be allowed to play at the bus stop anymore."

Charlie ignored the jokes and sat down.

"I'm *sooo* cold," she said to her friend Diane Slovy. "It's not even Halloween yet. But it feels like Christmas out there."

"Out there?" said Diane. "It's even colder *in here*. They must bring this creepy old wreck of a bus down from the North Pole every morning."

"This has to be the oldest bus in the world," said Charlie. "It's a wonder we get to school every day."

"I bet this bus is a hundred years old," said Derek James, a third grader who sat two rows in front of Charlie.

"There weren't any buses a hundred years ago, you dummy," said Brian.

"Yes, there were," said Derek. "And this bus is proof."

The bus sputtered and choked as it climbed a steep hill. It was only a week ago that the bus had been in the repair shop. Charlie was sure it was time for more repairs.

Three stops later, the bus arrived at Max Bollen's stop. Charlie and Max were best friends and they always sat together on the bus.

"This bus is in bad shape," said Max as he sat down. "It always screeches when it reaches the bus stop, but today it sounds like it's in pain."

"Derek says the bus is a hundred years old," said Diane.

"Buses have only been around about eighty years," replied Max.

"Well," said Derek. "This bus must be eighty years old."

"Wow," said Nadine Dudley. "Think of all the kids who have ridden on it."

"Those kids must be really old by now," said Prissy Vanderbilt, a third grader who sat near the front of the bus. "They might even be—DEAD."

"That's right," said Brian. "And now those kids are GHOSTS who are going to haunt *you*, Prissy."

"Very funny," said Prissy. "But you also ride this bus, Brian. That means that you could be haunted, too."

"But you're the only one who sits in the ghost chair," Brian said. "See that mark on the back of the seat? It's a ghost symbol. The girl who used to sit in your seat died of a broken heart, because the boy she liked always ripped up the love letters she sent him. Just like Howie Stern rips up yours. Anyone who sits in that seat is doomed to suffer the same fate as that girl."

"Anyone who sits in that seat is doomed to listen to your dumb stories, Brian," said Nadine. "That's scarier than any ghost."

"Wait a minute, you guys," said Marie Nast. "I don't know why you think ghosts are so funny. There's a haunted house in this town, and everyone knows it. It's that old mansion on Raven Lane that they were going to tear down. There was just an article about it in the paper. They found two graves in the yard."

"You're wrong about the Van Arpel house," said an older girl named Janice who had recently moved to town. "It's not haunted. It's just an old house."

Marie looked angry. "How do you know?" she growled. "You've only lived here for two weeks."

"Because I don't believe in haunted houses, and I don't believe in ghosts," said

Janice. "You and Brian are just trying to scare the other kids."

Clyde Fritz stood up. "I have something to say," he said.

"Have you seen a ghost?" asked Marie.

"No," said Clyde. "But . . ."

"But what?" said Prissy, who was still wondering if she was sitting in a haunted seat.

"I want to tell you about something *really* scary," said Clyde. "It's . . . it's . . ."

"Tell us!" yelled Prissy.

"It's . . . Marvin time!!!" yelled Clyde.

CHAPTER 2

The kids looked out the window. Marvin Kittleman was standing at the corner with his mother.

He was dressed in a bulky winter coat, a ski mask, heavy gloves, and snow shoes. Two scarves were wrapped around his neck.

Most of the kids started to clap their hands. "Marvin! Marvin! Marvin!" they yelled.

Max nudged Charlie. "I don't believe this," he said.

"You mean the way Marvin's dressed?" asked Charlie.

"Not just that," answered Max. "Look at where his mother's standing. She's trying to block the wind. Can you believe how weird she is? She's protecting Marvin from the wind!"

The bus screeched as it slowed to a stop.

8

Harry opened the door, and Marvin started up the steps.

"Hold on to the rail, dear," said Mrs. Kittleman. "I'm right behind you."

Marvin clumped up the steps and plopped down in his seat.

"Hello, Mrs. Kittleman," said Harry.

"It's cold in here," snapped Mrs. Kittleman. "Turn on the heat."

"The heat *is* on," said Harry. "It just doesn't work very well."

"It doesn't work at all," said Mrs. Kittleman. "It's actually colder in here than it is outside."

"You noticed that, too," said Harry. He chuckled. "Well there's nothing like a nice morning chill to start the day off right."

"That's not funny," said Mrs. Kittleman.

"Of course it's not," said Harry, trying to hide his smile. "Have a nice day, Mrs. Kittleman."

Mrs. Kittleman gave Harry a sour look and climbed down the steps. Harry stepped on the gas pedal. The engine made a funny wheezing noise, and the bus jounced forward.

"I'm hungry," said Brian. He took out his

lunch bag and looked inside. "Another stupid cucumber sandwich. That's all I ever get. I hate cucumbers."

Brian grabbed Prissy's shoulder. Prissy gasped.

"Don't be afraid, Prissy," said Brian. "I'm not the ghost. I'm your friend. I'm here to protect you."

"I don't need *your* protection, Brian," said Prissy, "and I don't believe in ghosts."

"You do need my protection," said Brian, "and all you have to do is trade me your dessert for my cucumber sandwich."

Prissy *was* afraid of the ghost, but she didn't want to admit it. She knew that everyone would laugh at her.

"Cucumber sandwiches?" she said. "I love cucumber sandwiches. All I ever get for dessert is yucky chocolate cake. Let's trade every day."

Brian smiled and handed his sandwich to Prissy. Then Prissy handed her cake to Brian.

Brian opened the wrapper and tried to stuff a large piece of cake in his mouth. Crumbs fell all over the floor.

"Brian Ray," said Janice, "you're totally

gross. You eat like a pig, and you don't even wait for lunch."

"Why should I wait?" said Brian. "I want it now. Besides, I can't ward off ghosts when I'm hungry."

"Well if he's going to eat his dessert now, so am I," said Clyde Fritz.

"Me, too," said Derek.

"Hey, I think I've started something here," said Brian. "From now on, we'll eat part of our lunches on the way to school. Then we'll do a chant to scare off the ghost that's haunting Prissy."

"That sounds like fun," said Derek. "But we don't know any chants."

"Leave that part to me," said Brian. "I'll go to the library and read a book about ghosts."

"This is crazy," whispered Charlie to Max. "We're supposed to protect Prissy from a ghost that Brian made up ten minutes ago."

"Don't worry about it," said Max. "It's just for fun. What I don't like is everyone eating their lunches on the bus. The oldest, creakiest bus in the world will soon be the smelliest bus, too."

The bus pulled into the school parking lot and stopped. Charlie picked up her backpack and started down the aisle. She was so cold that she could hardly move her fingers.

When she stepped off the bus, she was surprised to find that it really was colder on the bus than it was outside.

This is strange, she thought. *I wonder if a bus can have ghosts.*

CHAPTER 3

It was Current Events Day in Ms. Greig's third-grade class. Each of the students had to cut an article out of the local paper and give an oral report.

Charlie had cut out a news story about the election of a new mayor. The elections were two weeks away, and both candidates were going door to door, talking to voters.

Charlie liked her story and hoped that Ms. Greig would call on her first. She practiced what she was going to say while waiting for class to begin.

"Let's get right to our reports," said Ms. Greig as soon as she had taken attendance. "I'd like for Tony Totini to go first."

Tony made his way to the front of the classroom.

"My report is about the old Van Arpel mansion on Raven Lane. It says in the paper that the mansion is one of the oldest houses in town. It was built in 1893 by Cornelius Van Arpel, a very rich man who donated money that helped to build the town's library and first high school."

Tony continued. "The newspaper says that the house is in bad shape and can't be lived in anymore. The school bus parking garage is next door to the house. The school district bought the house and wants to tear it down and build a bigger garage."

Tony paused to make sure everyone was listening to him. "The really strange part of this story," he went on, "is that jewels and money have been found in the home by cleanup crews. And under the weeds in the yard, two graves have been uncovered. No one knows who's buried in them."

"That's very interesting, Tony," said Ms. Greig. "Does anyone have any questions?"

Alice Wiczer raised her hand. "How long has the house been vacant, and who was the last person to live there?"

Tony looked down at the newspaper. "It says that the house has been vacant for almost twenty years. The last people to live in the mansion were Mr. Van Arpel's two daughters. They were very old when they died, and they kept to themselves."

"Maybe the two daughters are buried in the graves," said Derek.

"Who knows," replied Tony. "The headstones don't have any names."

"I was telling some of the kids on my bus about that house on the way to school," said Marie. "I've heard it's haunted by ghosts."

"Well it sure *looks* spooky," said Tony. "There's a picture of the house in the newspaper."

"Pass that around so the other students can look at it," said Ms. Greig.

Tony handed the newspaper to Prissy, who was sitting in the first row.

"Oooh," she said. "That's a haunted house, all right."

Ms. Greig frowned. "I hope that none of you really believe that the Van Arpel mansion is haunted. I know it's easy to believe that an old abandoned house has ghosts. But the only things that you'd find at that house are old furniture, broken glass, spider webs, and rusty nails."

"And two graves," said Clyde.

"And two graves," said Ms. Greig.

CHAPTER 4

It was cold and windy the next morning as Charlie walked to the bus stop.

This time Charlie was ready. She was wearing a heavy coat, scarf, and warm gloves.

"Go ahead, wind," she said. "Blow as hard as you want. I can take it."

When the bus arrived, Charlie heard it make a terrible screaming noise. It was almost as though the bus were alive. Charlie shivered despite her warm clothes. *Maybe it's filled with the spirits of the dead,* she thought.

But when the bus door opened, she looked up and saw Harry smiling at her. As she climbed the steps, she heard lots of shouting from the other kids.

"Hello, little lady," said Harry. "Welcome to the noisiest bus in town."

"Why is everybody yelling?" asked Charlie.

"I don't know, and I don't care," said Harry. "I get paid to drive the bus. I'm not here to be a baby-sitter."

"But doesn't the noise drive you crazy?" asked Charlie.

"Not anymore," said Harry. "I'm wearing earplugs." Harry pointed to his ears.

"These things work great," said Harry. "This will be the first day this year that I don't go home with a headache."

Charlie smiled and started down the aisle.

"Did you say something, Charlie?" asked Harry.

Charlie turned back toward Harry.

"No, I didn't," she answered.

"What?" said Harry.

"NOTHING!" shouted Charlie.

"Good morning to you, too," said Harry.

Charlie shook her head and walked back to her seat.

"What's going on in here?" she asked as she sat down.

"Ghosts!" said Brian. "That's what's going on. When Clyde, Sam, and Diane got on the bus this morning, they found one of the windows open."

"But Harry always makes sure the windows are closed after he's dropped everyone off in the afternoon," said Charlie.

"That's right," said Brian. "So if Harry closes the windows, and windows don't open all by themselves, then Prissy's ghost must have come inside the bus last night."

"There's no ghost," said Charlie. "You made that whole story up to scare Prissy and get her dessert from her. The ghost's a fake."

"Don't say that!" said Brian. "You'll get the ghost mad! Then even *I* might not be able to protect Prissy. Are you willing to take that chance?"

"I sure am," said Charlie.

"I think you're both wrong," said Derek. "I think there are ghosts haunting this bus. But not Brian's ghost."

"Then what ghosts?" asked Charlie.

"Do you remember Tony's report about the Van Arpel mansion? He said the mansion is right next door to the school bus garage. And now they want to tear down the house to make the bus garage bigger. I think this bus is being haunted by the ghosts of the Van Arpel sisters. They're mad that their house is being torn down. And they're looking for revenge!"

19

"But what makes you so sure they would haunt our bus?" asked Charlie.

"I'm *not* sure," said Derek. "But some pretty strange things are going on around here. Like the window being open this morning. And the strange sounds this bus has been making the last few days. And why is it always colder *inside* the bus than outside?"

"I brought a book which has chants to ward off evil spirits," said Brian. "I think we should give it a try. But first, I need my chocolate cake."

Brian took out his cucumber sandwich and handed it to Prissy. Prissy handed her cake to Brian.

"Okay, everyone," said Brian. "This chant only works if we eat food before we chant. Everyone has to do it."

Brian took a big bite of cake. "Ummm, that's good," he said. "I like being a ghostbuster."

"Oh, brother," said Janice. "This is the stupidest thing I've ever seen. You can't scare a phony ghost by stuffing your faces with cake. My dessert is staying in the lunch bag until *I'm* ready to eat it—DURING LUNCH!"

"Me, too," said Charlie.

"But that'll ruin the chant," said Brian.

"That's too bad," said Janice. "Why don't you tell your phony ghosts to haunt Charlie and me instead of the bus."

"Hey, I like that," said Brian. "We'll send the ghosts to your houses. Just don't blame me if something bad happens."

CHAPTER 5

Brian opened a book of ghost chants.

"Let's see now," he said. "These chants are in alphabetical order. Ghosts in buildings . . . Ghosts in bumblebees . . . Ghosts in bunnies . . . Here it is. Ghosts in buses."

Brian stood up and read:

"To the ghosts who haunt this bus,
We demand that you listen to us.
Souls of the dead,
Spirits of the night.
Return to your graves,
And end our fright."

Brian closed the book. "If you have to haunt somebody, go to Janice's and Charlie's houses," he said.

The bus made a horrible screaming noise as it slowed down to pick up Max.

"Something's happening," said Brian. "I think the ghosts heard me."

"How will we know if the chant is working?" asked Diane.

"I'm not sure," said Brian. "The book doesn't say."

"I know," said Derek. "We'll leave the ghosts some food this afternoon on the way home. If the food's gone in the morning, we'll know that there are ghosts on this bus."

"They can have my cucumber sandwich," said Prissy.

"And they can have my chicken salad," said Clyde. "I hate chicken salad."

"We should also leave the ghosts a note," said Brian. "We'll ask the ghosts why they're haunting us."

"But what if the ghosts can't read?" asked Prissy.

"These are old ghosts," said Brian. "They've had plenty of time to learn how to read."

The bus stopped and Max got on.

"What's new?" he asked as he came down the aisle.

"We're being stupid today," said Janice. "We're reading ghost chants and eating cake and cookies for breakfast, and now we're turning the bus into a lunchroom for ghosts."

"Sounds like a normal day on *this* bus," said Max.

Max sat down next to Charlie.

"Let's practice for our spelling test," he said.

Charlie and Max opened their notebooks. Charlie was glad to be doing something other than thinking about ghosts. She didn't believe in ghosts—not really, anyway. But what if the bus really was haunted? And what if the ghosts had listened to Brian? And what would she do if the ghosts came to her house that night?

CHAPTER 6

It was 9:00 at night when Charlie heard a tap on her bedroom window. She had been sleeping. At first she thought it was the wind. But then she heard the noise a second time.

Charlie jumped out of bed.

What was that?! she thought. *Could it be a ghost?*

The tapping noise started again.

Charlie was scared. She wanted to open the curtains and look out the window, but she was too afraid.

"Grrrrrr" came a noise from outside.

Charlie was now panicking. "What'll I do? What'll I do?" she said over and over.

"Grrrrrr" the noise sounded again.

Charlie tried to remember Brian's chant. "To the ghosts who haunt this bus," she stammered. "We demand you . . . demand you . . . demand you . . . I can't remember!"

"Grrrrrr" went the noise for a third time.

Charlie was now so scared that she ran out of the room as fast as she could. She bolted down the steps and into the living room.

Her parents were watching TV.

"What's wrong, Charlotte?" asked her father. "You look like you've seen a ghost."

"I have!" said Charlie. "It's right outside my window."

Charlie's mother shook her head. "Bad dreams, again," she said. "This happens every time you eat baloney sandwiches before bedtime. You go to bed, you get sick, and you have nightmares."

"But this isn't a nightmare," said Charlie. "There's a ghost outside the house."

Charlie turned down the volume on the TV.

"Charlotte!" said Charlie's mother. "That's very rude of you. You should ask permission before you do that."

"I'm sorry," said Charlie, "but you have to hear the ghost."

"All right, all right. We're listening," said Charlie's father.

"Grrrrrr."

"That's it," said Charlie. "That's the ghost."

"It's probably just a dog," said Charlie's father. "I'll check on it, though. Let me get my coat and a flashlight."

Charlie's father left the room and went outside.

"Charlotte," said Charlie's mother, "we've told you many times that ghosts don't really exist. Why are you so sure that it's a ghost making these noises?"

Charlie told her mother about the bus, the Van Arpel house, and how Brian told the ghosts to go to Charlie's house.

"Well, I can see why you're scared," said Charlie's mother, "but you have to trust me on this one—there are no ghosts."

Charlie's mother gave Charlie a hug. "Nothing's going to hurt you," she said.

"Hey, you two," yelled Charlie's father. "I think I found Charlotte's ghost."

Charlie and her mother put on jackets and went outside. Charlie's father was standing on the front lawn with a flashlight in his hand.

"As soon as I stepped outside, I saw a boy

with blond hair scrambling down the tree near your window, Charlotte. He ran away from the house," he said.

Charlie's father pointed his flashlight toward the ground.

"Somebody left some chewing gum on the lawn," he said. "It's probably the same kid I saw running away. I think someone is playing a trick on you, Charlotte."

"And I think I know who's doing it, too," said Charlie.

CHAPTER 7

It was much warmer the next day as Charlie waited for the bus. The sun was out, and it was nice to be able to leave her coat and gloves at home.

Charlie was also happy to know that Brian's ghost wasn't a ghost after all. It was Brian who had been outside her window the night before.

The bus rolled up to Charlie's stop. It made the same screaming noise that it had made the past two days. Brian's ghost chant hadn't stopped the funny noise.

Charlie got on the bus and went back to her seat. She noticed that the kids were just as noisy today as they had been yesterday.

"What's going on?" she asked Diane as she sat down.

"More strange stuff," said Diane. "Remember how we left food and a note on the bus yesterday afternoon?"

Charlie nodded.

"Well, when we got on the bus this morning, we found one of the windows open. The food we left on the bus was gone, and the note was scrunched up."

"Maybe someone cleaned the bus last night," said Charlie.

"No," said Diane. "Whoever or *whatever* took the food tore open the bags the food was in. The bags were all over the floor this morning."

"I think Brian's doing this," whispered Charlie. "He was outside my house last night, pretending to be a ghost."

"Are you sure it was him?" asked Diane.

"I'm pretty sure," said Charlie. "My dad saw someone who looked like Brian running away from the house."

"But how could Brian be doing things to the bus?" asked Diane.

"I'm not sure," said Charlie. "But I just *know* he's behind all of this ghost stuff."

Brian stood up. "Last night I learned some new ghostbusting chants in my book.

But while I was practicing them, the three ghosts came into my bedroom."

"Three?" gulped Prissy.

"Yes," said Brian. "The two Van Arpel sisters and the girl who died of a broken heart. They said that the hauntings are a warning."

"A warning?" said Derek. "What are they warning us about?"

"They said that if the Van Arpel house is torn down, they will come for revenge."

"But what can *we* do about that?" asked Prissy.

"We have to show the ghosts that we mean business. I have a whole bunch of new chants today. But first, it's time to eat!"

Brian and Prissy traded food again while most of the other kids opened up their desserts. When Max got on the bus, almost everyone was eating.

"Looks like Brian's trying to scare ghosts again," he said as he sat down.

"Brian's not trying to scare ghosts," said Charlie. "He's trying to scare the kids who ride this bus."

Charlie told Max about all the things that had happened overnight.

"Boy," said Max, "that sounds strange.

Not even Brian could break into this bus at night. Something else must be going on."

"So you think there *are* ghosts?" asked Charlie.

"I didn't say that," replied Max. "I'm not sure what to think."

Brian opened his book and started a new chant.

"I know one thing," said Charlie. "Whatever's going on, Brian is making worse. He's starting to scare some of the little kids."

The bus slowed down as it reached Marvin Kittleman's stop. Again, it made a loud screaming noise.

The door opened and Marvin climbed up the steps. His mother was right behind him.

"I'm very upset at you, Harry," she said.

"What?" said Harry. He was still wearing his earplugs.

"Marvin's been coming home crying about ghosts on the bus. He's scared to death!"

Harry pulled one of his earplugs out. "Why would Marvin be afraid of toast on the bus?"

"NOT *TOAST!*" yelled Mrs. Kittleman. "GHOSTS!"

"No need to yell," said Harry. "I heard you. But why would Marvin think there are ghosts on this bus?"

"How could you be asking me that kind of question?" said Mrs. Kittleman. "You sit here every day while the kids on this bus do weird chants and offer their lunches to ghosts. How come you don't know what goes on in your own bus?"

Harry shrugged. "It's not that I don't know . . . it's . . . well . . . are you sure the kids have been doing chants?"

Mrs. Kittleman rolled her eyes. "You don't know what goes on in here, do you? There could be a fire on this bus and you wouldn't know about it until *your* seat was burning. Well, if I hear about any more ghosts on this bus, I'm going to haunt you!"

Mrs. Kittleman turned around and stormed off.

Harry closed the door and stood up.

"I'm not a happy guy right now," he said. "And I have a rule. When I'm not happy, you kids can't be happy either. When I find out who's the joker behind all of this, that person's going to be even less happy than the rest of us."

CHAPTER 8

Things did not go well for Brian that day. Harry made him sit in the front row of the bus. Brian had to repeat over and over, "There are no ghosts on this bus. There never were any ghosts. There'll never be any ghosts. And if there were ghosts, Harry would protect us from them."

Harry made Brian say those lines all the way to school and then all the way home. It seemed that Brian's ghost chants were over for good.

When Charlie boarded the bus the next morning, everything looked as if it were back to normal. The bus was quiet, and Harry was in a better mood. Charlie noticed that he wasn't wearing his earplugs.

But as Charlie made her way back to her seat, she noticed that some of the kids looked worried.

Then Charlie saw that Diane was sitting in Charlie's seat. And she looked more scared than anyone else.

"I'm so glad you're here, Charlie," Diane shrieked. She got up to let Charlie sit down and moved to Max's seat. "I've never been this scared in my life!"

"What's wrong?" asked Charlie.

"When I got on the bus this morning, the window that we found open yesterday—was open again. But that's not the bad part."

"Tell me," said Charlie.

"Okay," said Diane. "But promise me you won't scream."

"I promise," said Charlie.

"There is a pile of b-b-bones in front of my seat, Charlie."

"Bones?" said Charlie. "What do you mean?"

"I mean there are bones under the seat in front of mine. Derek thinks they came from one of the graves at the Van Arpel house. And I'm freaking out."

"Maybe Brian put them there to scare us," said Charlie.

"Not the way he's acting this morning," said Diane. She pointed to where Brian was sitting, four rows in front. "He's so scared, I can see him shaking from here."

"There *has* to be a reason for this," said Charlie. "And when Max gets here, I'm sure he'll tell us what it is. Until then, I don't want to look at those bones."

A few minutes later, the bus reached Max's stop. Max was surprised to find Diane sitting in his seat.

"Are you guys playing musical chairs?" he asked. "If Diane's taking my seat, then I'll sit in Diane's seat."

"No! Don't sit there!" screamed Charlie and Diane.

But Max sat down in the seat anyway. "You two are weird," he said as he took off his backpack.

"You don't understand," said Charlie. "There's a pile of bones under the seat in front of you. They could belong to a dead person. They were here this morning when Diane sat down. And the same window as yesterday was open."

Max shook his head. "Grow up, you guys. Some kid probably ate chicken legs on the bus and threw the bones under the seat. Let me have a look."

Max bent over and looked under the seat in front of him.

"YIKES!!" he shouted. "They're huge!!!"

Max grabbed his backpack and jumped to the seat across the aisle.

"What do you think it is?" asked Charlie. "And how did they get on the bus?"

"I don't know, and I don't want to know," said Diane. "I never believed in ghosts before, but those bones give me the creeps."

"They've got to be from the haunted house," said Marie. "This bus is haunted for sure."

"It could be," said Max. "There's only one way to find out for sure. It might be dangerous though."

Diane cringed. "If it's dangerous, count me out."

"I plan to do this job alone," said Max. "I'm going to the bus garage after school to find out what's really going on."

"Are you crazy?" said Marie. "If the ghosts are haunting the garage, you don't stand a chance alone against them."

"Then I'll go, too," said Charlie. "Those ghosts will have to take on both of us."

"Those ghosts are already taking on this

whole bus," said Marie. "And we're a long way from the haunted house. You'll be two kids taking on those ghosts in their own backyard."

"Well," said Charlie. "I'm not scared."

But she was.

CHAPTER 9

All through the day, Charlie worried about what would happen to her and Max at the garage. She hoped that Max would change his mind about going. But Max was determined to go, and there was no way that Charlie would let him go alone.

Soon school was over. Max and Charlie put together their plan on the way to their bus.

"We'll both get off the bus at my stop," said Max. "It's closer to the bus garage, so we won't have to walk as far."

Charlie nodded. "We'll hang out at my house for a while," Max went on. "We don't want to get to the garage until after it closes. You can call your mother from my house and tell her you're with me."

"I'll tell her I'll be home in time for supper," Charlie said.

"Good. Then when we reach the haunted —I mean Van Arpel—mansion, we'll look around outside," said Max. "I don't want to go inside that house unless we see something strange. What do you think, Charlie?"

Charlie didn't have to think about going inside at all. She didn't want to be in the same town as the Van Arpel house. And the last thing she wanted was to be *inside* the house. But Charlie wanted to *act* brave even if she didn't *feel* brave.

"I think you're right," she said. "We shouldn't go inside the house unless there's a really good reason."

"I'm glad we agree," said Max. "So after we look around the outside of the house, we'll go straight to the bus garage."

"And look around the outside," said Charlie.

Max seemed surprised. "You don't want to go inside the bus garage?" he asked. "I thought that was the whole idea of doing this."

"Of course it is," said Charlie. "I just thought we'd look around outside *before* going inside."

By now, Charlie and Max had reached the

bus. Brian was standing by the door, talking to his friends, Rapper and Mickey.

He was trying to convince his friends that the bus was haunted. But they didn't believe him. All week he had bragged to them about how he had made up a ghost story to get Prissy's desserts. They also knew that he had gone over to Charlie's house two nights ago to try and scare her.

"Brian," said Rapper, "how stupid do you think we are? You scared all those punky kids on the bus, and that's cool. But we're too smart for this game. Save your breath."

"This is different," said Brian. "I didn't break into the bus at night. I didn't put those bones inside. This ghost business is for real."

"Oh yeah?" said Mickey. "Prove it. If you want us to believe you, then we need to see a picture of your ghosts."

"How do you expect me to do that?" asked Brian. "Am I supposed to call them up and ask them over to my house?"

"To get a picture of ghosts," said Mickey, "you have to go to *their* house."

"That's right," said Rapper. "You go over to your haunted house and wait for your ghostie friends to come out. Follow them over to the bus garage. When they open the bus window, take their picture."

Brian cringed. "I don't know about this," he said shyly.

"You're totally chicken," snapped Rapper. "I don't know why I hang out with you."

"I'm not chicken," said Brian. "And I'm not afraid of ghosts. I'll go down to that house and get pictures of them. But I won't show them to you two clowns. I'll take them to the newspaper. Then I'll be rich and famous. And when you guys come crawling on your hands and knees for money, I'll just laugh at you."

"Unless the ghosts get you first," said Rapper.

CHAPTER 10

Charlie and Max spent most of the afternoon at Max's house.

"I've always wanted to be a spy," Max said, excitedly. "Like James Bond, 007. If we solve this case, we could go into the spy business together. You could be 'Charlie Sleuth, Agent 008' of the 'Max and Charlie Undercover Agency'."

"I'd rather be Charlie McKee, boring third-grade girl who stays out of trouble, haunted houses, and spooky bus garages."

Max frowned. "Are you saying that you don't want to poke around the garage with me?"

"Sure I do," said Charlie. "But what'll you do if we run into ghosts?"

"There aren't any ghosts there," said Max, shaking his head. "I promise."

Charlie was glad that Max was so sure of

himself. She only wished that she could be as sure as he was.

"It's 4:30," said Max. "Time to go."

Charlie and Max put on their sweaters and started out for the bus garage. It was beginning to get dark and the wind was blowing. Charlie was feeling creepy.

"It's cold, windy, and gloomy," said Max. "Perfect weather for spying."

Perfect weather for ghosts, thought Charlie.

The Van Arpel mansion was in a very old section of town. Most of the homes had been built at the turn of the century. Many now looked shabby.

Even the trees looked older than in other places. Their branches were large and bare. Clumps of brown leaves covered the sidewalk.

Charlie and Max reached Raven Lane and walked toward the Van Arpel mansion. Charlie started to slow down. Her legs seemed to be sensing danger. But Max was walking faster than before. It looked to Charlie as if he were being drawn toward the house.

"Come on, slowpoke," he said. "The fun's about to begin."

As they approached the house, Charlie

was surprised to see just how run-down it was. The whole place looked battered and weather-worn. Most of the windows were broken. Brown weeds grew waist high in the front yard and garbage was strewn everywhere.

"Awesome!" said Max. "We should go inside and check this out."

"No!" shouted Charlie. "What I mean is that we agreed to go inside only if there was a good reason. I think we should stick to our plan."

"Let's just look in a window," said Max.

Max started to make his way through the weeds.

"Stop!" said Charlie.

But Max kept going.

"Yuck!" he said as he reached one of the front windows.

"What is it?" asked Charlie.

"Cobwebs," said Max. "I have cobwebs all over me."

"What about the inside of the house?" asked Charlie. "Can you see anything?"

"It's too dark," said Max.

Slowly Charlie made her way to the win-

dow. "There's something moving in there!" she whispered.

"It's your imagination," Max said. "Let's go to the back of the yard and see what we can find."

"Don't go *there!*" Charlie yelled. "That's where the graves are."

"Wait here and make sure I come back," Max said.

A minute later Max called out to Charlie. "I see the graves. There's something chiseled on one of the headstones."

"But the newspaper article said there weren't any names on the headstones," Charlie said as she walked in Max's direction.

"There aren't. This is some sort of mark or symbol."

"A mark or symbol?" said Charlie. "That's totally spooky. It could mean *anything!* Let's get out of here while we can."

Charlie started to run.

Max ran after her. "Stop!" he said. "We're supposed to go to the bus garage, remember?"

"Okay," said Charlie. "At least there aren't any graves there."

Charlie and Max walked away from the Van Arpel house. The bus garage was right next door. Old warehouses and stores lined the rest of the street.

There was a restaurant on the other side of the garage.

"We have to be very careful," said Max. "We don't want anyone in the restaurant to see us."

Charlie and Max sneaked around the outside of the garage. The building was bad smelling, dank, and oily. A row of garbage cans on one side of the building added to the bad smell.

Max and Charlie peeked in some of the windows, trying to locate their bus.

"How are we going to find our bus?" Charlie asked. "It's so dark in there. I wish we had a flashlight."

"We have to find a way in," said Max. "Look! There's a hole by the ground where some of the bricks have fallen out."

"We're too big to fit in that," said Charlie.

"Then we have to look for an unlocked door," said Max. "And there's not much chance of that."

"That's too bad," said Charlie, although she was secretly glad. The last place Charlie wanted to be was inside a haunted bus garage.

Max walked over to a side door and tried the doorknob. To his surprise, the door was unlocked. It made a strange crying noise as Max opened it. The noise reminded Charlie of the noise the bus had been making.

Charlie was scared. She could hardly move her feet.

"Hurry up and come inside," whispered Max.

Charlie tiptoed into the garage. Then Max let go of the door.

Now Charlie and Max were alone—in the dark.

CHAPTER 11

I'm going to be a hero, thought Brian, as he rode his bicycle toward the Van Arpel house.

Brian had brought his camera with him. He planned to take a picture of the ghosts and leave as quickly as he could.

But as Brian reached Raven Lane, he could feel his heart starting to pound.

Maybe I shouldn't do this, he thought. *But then, everyone will think I'm a chicken. Besides, all I need is one picture.*

Brian rode up to the Van Arpel house and parked his bike in front. He walked around the front yard, picking his way through garbage and broken glass.

He stepped up on the front porch and tried the front door.

"Locked!" he said, almost relieved. "I guess there's no way in. Well, at least I tried."

Brian decided to take some pictures of the house.

"This will be proof to those losers that I at least *tried* to get in. Then I'll go to the bus garage and do the same thing. I'll try one door. If it doesn't open, I'll take pictures of the garage and leave."

Brian aimed his camera at the outside of the Van Arpel mansion. The flashbulb lit up the side of the house as he took the picture.

Brian took three more pictures from different angles.

I'm doing great, he thought. *I feel brave. Hey, maybe I'll go take a picture of the* graves. *That'll really impress everybody.*

Brian made his way to the graves. *I'll just take a nice shot of the headstones,* he thought.

Brian bent down. Suddenly he shuddered. "No! It can't be," he yelled. "One of these headstones has a mark in it. And the mark looks exactly like that stupid scratch on the back of Prissy's seat on the bus. I told Prissy it was a ghost symbol, and she believed me. Maybe it *is* a ghost symbol. Now maybe somebody or something's out to get *me.*"

Brian ran back to his bicycle.

"I wanna go home," he moaned. "But I have to go to the bus garage and take pictures. The faster I do it, the faster I can go home."

Brian peddled his bicycle over to the garage and parked it next to the same door Charlie and Max had gone through earlier.

"I'll make this look really good," thought Brian. "I'll take a picture of the buses parked inside. But I'll do it through a window. With my camera flash the picture should come out."

Brian walked over to the window and aimed his camera. As he snapped the button on his camera, the flashbulb went off. Some of the light bounced off the window and flashed in his eyes.

"Ouch," said Brian, blinking.

Then he walked over to the door and turned the knob.

"Just my luck," he thought. "The stupid thing's unlocked."

Brian opened the door. It made the same strange crying noise as it had when Max had opened it. Brian let go of the door, and it slammed shut.

Now he was really scared. "Oh please, let me live," he whispered under his breath. "I promise to be good from now on."

Brian walked forward slowly. The garage was quiet, except for a steady dripping noise.

Then he heard whispering sounds.

The ghosts! he thought.

Brian was terrified. He wanted to run out of the building as fast as he could. But then he remembered why he was there.

"I'm here to prove that these ghosts exist. I'm here to be a hero," he muttered.

Brian grabbed his camera with both hands and tried to walk toward the voices. Then the whispering stopped.

Brian walked slowly forward in the dark. *This must be a trap,* he told himself. *If only I wasn't so brave.*

BANG!!! came a loud noise.

"Ahhhh!!!" hollered Brian, now scared to death. He ran as fast as he could toward the door, but he tripped over an object that had been left on the floor. He hit the ground hard, breaking his camera.

Trying to pick himself up, he saw two yellowish eyes reflecting in the light from a nearby window.

"No!!!" he hollered as he tried to get away.

Brian stood up, expecting something to happen at any moment. Then he looked around, searching for the terrible yellow eyes, but there was no sign of the eyes or any ghosts. So Brian limped as fast as he could to the doorway.

As Brian opened the door, he thought he felt a ghostlike presence sending chills down his back. The door made a screaming noise as it slammed shut behind him.

Free! I'm out of there! Brian breathed to himself.

Suddenly he tripped over the garbage cans that were next to the door. The cans came crashing down.

Brian got up on his feet and ran as fast as he could.

CHAPTER 12

"We've got to get out of here," said Max. "This place *is* haunted. First we saw that flash of light through the window. Then we heard the door open. Then the banging and the hollering sounds. Then more crashing, hollering, and screaming. This place is *totally* haunted."

"I'm with you," said Charlie. "Let's make a run for the door."

Charlie and Max got up and made their way to the door. Once outside, they noticed that the garbage cans had been knocked over and that there was now a bicycle parked next to the building.

"I don't remember seeing that bicycle before," said Max as they ran from the building.

"It's probably a ghost bicycle," said Charlie. "I don't want to go near it."

"It's getting late," said Max. "Our folks are worried about us for sure."

"They should be worried," said Charlie. *"I'm* worried about us."

"Just don't tell them what you've been doing," said Max.

"You mean that I've been hanging out in a haunted bus garage with the ghosts of the Van Arpel sisters?" said Charlie. "They wouldn't believe it anyway."

When Charlie got on the bus the next morning, she saw a large group of kids gathered around Brian. He was talking softly.

"What's going on here?" asked Charlie.

"Not so loud," whispered Brian. "I don't want Harry to hear us. But I'm sure now that the bus is haunted. I was in the bus garage last night, and I saw one of the ghosts."

"YOU WERE IN THE GARAGE LAST NIGHT?" yelled Charlie.

"Sshhh!" whispered Brian. "I know it was crazy for me to go. But I thought it was my duty to protect the kids on this bus from the ghosts."

"Anyway," he continued. "I heard them whispering to me. Then one of them grabbed me. I fought with all my strength, but it knocked me to the ground and broke my camera. And then . . ."

"Yes?"

"And then I saw its eyes! They were yellow and evil. I just freaked out after that. I ran out the door and knocked over some garbage cans. I was so scared that I even left my bicycle there."

Charlie now knew that it was Brian who'd made all the noises in the bus garage. She felt relieved as she went back to her seat.

When Max got on the bus, she told him that Brian had actually been in the garage with them.

Max started to laugh. "It was Brian? Not a ghost? So that part's solved. But we still don't know who or what has been breaking into the bus."

CHAPTER 13

Charlie was puzzled. She felt sure that there were no ghosts in the garage or on the bus. Still, strange things were happening. Things that could not be explained.

Maybe Brian was behind it all. Maybe he was sneaking into the bus garage every night. Maybe he was doing it to scare the other kids. But last night, something scared Brian.

"Charlie, are you listening?" asked Ms. Greig.

Charlie sat up in her chair.

"I'm sorry," she said. "I was thinking about something."

"Please pay attention, Charlie," said Ms. Greig. "You won't learn anything if you don't listen."

But Charlie only wanted to learn about one thing. And she didn't think that today's lesson would tell her anything about how bones get on buses.

It was Current Events Day in class again. Alice Wiczer had been chosen to go first.

"My article is about raccoons," said Alice.

Some of the kids moaned. Charlie felt like moaning, but she didn't want to be rude.

Alice frowned. "Okay," she said, "my article is about *super* raccoons. The newspaper says that the police are finding more raccoons around here than ever before."

"That's not super," said Clyde. "*Superman* can fly. What can these raccoons do?"

Alice looked nervous. "Well," she said, "it doesn't say anything about flying raccoons. But they have been knocking over garbage cans, opening screen doors, and even going inside people's houses. It says they'll do anything to get food."

Clyde raised his hand. "What do they look like?" he asked. "Do they wear capes like Superman?"

"That's enough, Clyde," scolded Ms. Greig. "I happen to think that this is a very interesting topic."

Alice continued. "According to the article, the raccoons have very sharp noses and yellow eyes that shine in the dark. They have bushy ringed tails . . . but no capes. These raccoons use their front paws to open doors, push down windows, unwrap packages, and throw food all over the place. One lady says that they leave a trail of crumpled paper and make awful noises when they knock over stuff."

"I haven't seen any raccoons yet," said Tony. "But I'd like to."

"So would I," said Alice. "The raccoons are being seen just about everywhere in town, especially in one neighborhood."

"Which neighborhood is that?" asked Ms. Greig.

"It's in the oldest section of town," said Alice. "Over by the Van Arpel mansion."

"Does anyone in class live in that area of town?" asked Ms. Greig.

Nobody raised his hand.

Suddenly Charlie jumped up out of her chair.

"That's it!" she shouted. "I've solved the mystery!"

Ms. Greig looked sternly at Charlie. "I told you to pay attention, young lady. And I will not tolerate yelling in the classroom."

"But I *have* been listening," said Charlie. "And because of Alice, I've solved the mystery of the haunted bus."

Alice smiled. "Glad to help," she said. "But what did I do?"

"I'd better start at the beginning," said Charlie. "Weird things have been happening on our bus. In the morning we've found open windows, and food missing, and even crumpled-up pieces of paper."

The kids who rode Charlie's bus nodded in agreement.

"Last night Max and I went down to the bus garage to look for a clue to the mystery," Charlie went on. "We found a row of garbage cans—garbage cans that would attract any raccoons in the area. And Alice said that many raccoons have been spotted around that part of town.

"There's a hole in the building near where our bus is parked. A raccoon could easily fit through that hole. Once inside the garage, he'd smell the food that we've been leaving on the bus these past few days. Then he'd use his front paws to open the window."

"That makes sense," said Derek. "And Brian said that his ghost had yellow eyes.

The raccoons have yellow eyes. Big, tough Brian's been scared to death by a raccoon."

"But the *bones*—what about the bones?" asked Prissy. "How do we know they didn't come from the graves?"

"Maybe I can help with that," said Ms. Greig. "Those of you who've seen the bones can tell me what they looked like."

Max and the other kids from the bus took turns describing the bones. Then Ms. Greig took out a book on skeletons.

"Based on your descriptions, there's no *human* bone that looks anything like what you saw," she said.

Tony raised his hand. "It came from the garbage," he said. "Someone probably made a ham. My mom cooks ham with the bone in. And when she makes stew, she puts bones in for flavoring."

"So the raccoon found the bones in the garbage and took them into the bus to chew the meat off," said Max.

"That makes sense," said Charlie. "There's a restaurant next door to the garage. They must throw out plenty of bones."

"Let's write a letter to the newspaper giving them the facts about *our* raccoon story," said Ms. Greig. "We can make it a class project."

"I can't wait to tell Brian about this," said Derek. "I wonder if he has a chant for scaring off raccoons."

CHAPTER 14

Charlie stood at the bus stop and waited for her bus to come. The sky was gray again, and she shivered in the cold wind.

But today was Halloween. And Halloween was supposed to be cold and gloomy. Still, she'd rather be in a warm school building than at a cold bus stop.

Every year at Halloween, the kids on the bus wore costumes to school. This year, their theme was "School Bus Ghosts." Charlie was disguised as "Super Raccoon." She was wearing a raccoon mask, a furry coat and tail. She was also wearing a cape.

The bus pulled up.

S-C-R-E-E-C-H!!! E-E-E-C-H!!

The bus was now making its *normal* stopping noise. No more terrible screams.

The doors opened and Charlie climbed up the steps.

"No raccoons on the bus," growled Harry. "School regulations do not allow animals to ride to school."

"Very funny, Harry," said Charlie as she started down the aisle.

"I'm not kidding. You'll have to leave," said Harry.

"But I'm not really a raccoon," said Charlie. "It's just me, Charlie."

Harry smiled. "I know," he said. "I'm just teasing you. That's a great outfit you're wearing, little lady."

"The bus sounds better today," said Charlie.

"They repaired it yesterday after school," said Harry. "This bus is as good as new."

Charlie looked around. The bus still looked old and beat up. But it did *sound* better.

Charlie made her way toward her seat. She saw that most of the other kids were wearing costumes. Derek and Clyde were in ghost costumes. Prissy was dressed as the girl who died of a broken heart. She had a plastic heart hanging from her neck. It had been cut into two pieces.

The only two kids who hadn't dressed up

were Janice, who thought the whole thing was silly, and Brian, who still insisted that the bus was haunted. Every now and then he sneaked a glance at the back of Prissy's seat.

Charlie sat down behind Diane. Diane was wearing a drawing of a haunted house.

"I love your costume," said Charlie.

"I'm the Van Arpel mansion, and I'm for sale," Diane replied. She held up a "For Sale" sign. "I come complete with two graves, a year's supply of spider webs, and two angry ghosts."

"Sounds like a great buy," said Charlie.

"Did I mention the bats in the attic?" asked Diane. "They come with the house. No extra charge."

"Wow!" said Charlie. "Where do I sign?"

Three stops later, Max got on the bus.

"What are you wearing?" asked Charlie as Max reached his seat.

"I'm a book of ghost bus chants," said Max. "Open up the cover and look inside."

Charlie opened the large cardboard pieces that were Max's "book" cover.

"Surprise!" shouted Max.

"There's a newspaper inside your costume," said Charlie.

"This isn't just any newspaper. The front page is about us," said Max.

Charlie looked at the headline. It said, "Haunted School Bus Mystery Solved by Clever Detectives."

"We're in the paper!" shouted Charlie. "We're famous."

Charlie and the other kids took turns reading the newspaper article. Since the article was part of Max's costume, he had to move from seat to seat.

"I'm a hero!" said Brian. "That's what the paper says."

"No way," snarled Prissy. "You're just a troublemaker."

"Well the paper says I'm a *brave* troublemaker for going over to the Van Arpel mansion and the bus garage."

"Hey, everybody, it's Marvin time!" shouted Clyde.

"Marvin! Marvin! Marvin!" shouted most of the kids.

Harry shook his head in disgust.

"That's it," he groaned. "This is my last year with these kids."

S-C-R-E-E-C-H!!! E-E-E-C-H!!

Harry opened the door, and Marvin

started up the steps. As usual, he was wearing enough clothes to keep himself and two other people warm.

Mrs. Kittleman was right behind him. She did not look happy.

"Harry," she said. "I'm very upset with you."

"Looks like things are back to normal on this bus," said Max as he returned to his seat.

"Things are never normal on this bus," said Charlie.

About the Authors

MARJORIE WEINMAN SHARMAT, author of the classic *Nate the Great* series and numerous other books, is envious of the 16,525½ miles her son Andrew rode on school buses. She recalls trudging to school in the snow-covered streets of her native Maine. Mrs. Sharmat lives in Tucson with her husband, Mitchell. Their other son, Craig, is a veteran of the school-bus experience, but neglected to count the miles.

ANDREW SHARMAT, author of the highly praised picture-book, *Smedge*, claims to have logged 16,525½ miles riding school buses over the years in New York. In addition to being an author and bus rider, Mr. Sharmat is a professional real-estate appraiser. Hw grew up in New York and now lives with his wife, Lisa, in Tucson, Arizona.